PLAYS FOR PERFORMANCE

A series designed for
contemporary production and study
Edited by
Nicholas Rudall and Bernard Sahlins

CHRISTOPHER MARLOWE

Doctor Faustus

In a New Adaptation by
Nicholas Rudall

Ivan R. Dee
CHICAGO

Library of Congress Cataloging-in-Publication Data:
Rudall, Nicholas.
    Doctor Faustus : in a new adaptation /
    by Nicholas Rudall.
       p.   cm. — (Plays for performance)
    ISBN 0-929587-60-X (cloth : alk. paper).
    — ISBN 0-929587-56-1 (pbk. : alk. paper).
    1. Faust, d. ca. 1540—Drama. I. Marlowe, Christopher, 1564–1593. Doctor Faustus. II. Title. III. Series.
    PS3568.U299D6 1991
    812'.54—dc20   91-17073

INTRODUCTION
by Nicholas Rudall

This adaptation of *Doctor Faustus* is designed to create a text suitable for performance. It is well known that Marlowe's original text was the object of tampering almost immediately after the playwright's death. And there have been many attempts to reconstruct the original and to identify the spurious additions. This edition does not enter these important academic arguments; its express intent is to make the play available for performance. To that end I have excised many of the weakest comic scenes and rewritten or rearranged some of them in order to clarify their dramatic intent. I have also rearranged the order of some of the later serious scenes in the interest of narrative clarity. This text in fact evolved during the rehearsal process of a successful professional production.

Cast Size

It is possible, even desirable, to double various roles. For example:
Wagner and the Chorus
Valdes, Lucifer, The Pope, Knight
Cornelius, Belzebub, Emperor
Clown, Old Man
Good Angel, Helen of Troy, Nan Spit

3

Evil Angel, Scholar
The Seven Deadly Sins can be performed by
the entire company.

Stage Set

A desirable set would feature the principal ar-
chitectural components of an Elizabethan theatre.
There should be a down stage playing area that
can serve as Faustus's study and, with his desk
removed, all other external locales. Behind this
there could be an elevated playing area for the
comic scenes. Underneath this, corresponding to
the Elizabethan "inner below," there might be a
third area, perhaps partially covered in scrim,
through which Mephistophilis and the other appa-
ritions could appear.

Production Notes on the Individual Scenes

SCENE 1. The Latin: It is advisable to use the
given translations as part of the actual text. Most
of the time Marlowe supplies a translation following the Latin.

At the beginning of the scene Faustus rejects
actual books.

In our production the Good Angel and the
Evil Angel took the form of disembodied masks
lit behind the scrim.

I have divided the long monologues of Cornelius and Valdes between the two characters.

SCENE 2. A difficult little scene. Its dramatic
purpose is to show that Faustus is respected by his
fellow scholars and that they fear Cornelius and
Valdes. It also serves to show the comic side of
Wagner.

4

SCENE 3. I have translated most of the Latin of the original and put the English version into the text. It is a matter of judgment whether a director wishes to restore all the Latin.

The entrance of the first Devil affords a major opportunity for some quick visual pyrotechnics.

I chose not to have Mephistophilis enter as a friar. He was entirely steel blue and entered into a cross-shaped light pattern on the stage floor. A sudden, eerie entrance is obviously desirable. Scrim and back lighting help immensely.

SCENE 4. This comic scene should mirror the previous scene as deftly as possible.

The entrance of the two Devils offers another opportunity for masks, sound effects, firecrackers, rattles, and a light show.

SCENE 5. The beginning of the scene is self-explanatory. The most interesting section theatrically is the response to Mephistophilis' line "I'll fetch him somewhat to delight his mind." We chose to create a collage of visual projections which ranged from the face of Helen of Troy to images of the universe. It was accompanied by appropriately ethereal music.

The entrance of a "Devil dressed as a woman" allows the director to draw many of the visual connections suggested by the text. The "wife" should be played by the actress who will be Helen. But while suggesting Helen she should be a suddenly hideous form of her.

The books at the end of the scene should be magically given to Faustus by masked creatures.

SCENE 6. Clearly there is a passage of time between Scenes 5 and 6. We actually staged that passage of time, since within it Faustus has begun

5

to experience his newfound powers. We presented the illusion through lights and sound of Faustus "beholding the heavens," seeing the planets and the movement of the galaxies.

Lucifer and Belzebub perhaps are better left to as much of the audience's imagination as possible. Although they should be present on stage, they may be back lit and create huge shadows.

For the Seven Deadly Sins we created puppets, some huge, and worked with the company to represent the Sins. Pride was a Noblewoman with an arrogant nose. Covetousness was a puritan. Wrath was a red-faced judge. Envy was a huge green bishop. Gluttony was a large belching pig in uniform. Sloth was an academic wearing a mortar board and constantly yawning. Lechery looked, yet again, like a distortion of the actress playing Helen.

SCENE 7. At the beginning of this scene Faustus pours himself a drink of water from a clear decanter. Mephistophilis pours his own. It turned into wine.

The scene with the Pope is not very strong unless the director can create a magically movable feast. It is not quite theatrical enough for the "invisible" Faustus to do all the snatching of food. It is a nice touch if the friars have smoking censers.

SCENE 8. I have brought together a number of scenes and characters here. Nonetheless, it remains a very tricky comic scene. It needs a separate style. It cannot be deleted because it introduces Helen of Troy and serves as the main mechanism of revealing Faustus's powers.

Removing the Knight's horns is a challenge unless they are attached to wires.

The Empress is pregnant.

6

SCENE 9. This short passage allows Faustus to return to his study.

SCENE 10. This scene should show how the magic arts have descended to the lowest comic level. Nan Spit should again look like a debased version of Helen.

SCENE 11. The Old Man might be a friar.
Mephistophilis' appearance with the dagger should be astonishing. If Faustus has been given a symbol of power, e.g., a cloak, earlier in the play, it is very effective if Helen removes it. It is both appropriately erotic and suggestive of Faustus's imminent decline.

SCENE 12. All that is needed is a brilliant actor.

CHARACTERS

JOHN FAUSTUS, Doctor of Theology

VALDES
CORNELIUS } magicians, friends of Faustus

THREE SCHOLARS, friends of Faustus

AN OLD MAN

THE POPE

THE CARDINAL OF LORRAINE

CHARLES V, emperor of the Holy Roman
         Empire

EMPRESS

A KNIGHT

A GOOD ANGEL

AN EVIL ANGEL

MEPHISTOPHILIS

LUCIFER

BELZEBUB

THE SEVEN DEADLY SINS
ALEXANDER THE GREAT } spirits
HELEN OF TROY

WAGNER, servant to Faustus, and Chorus

A CLOWN

RALPH, a servingman

CHORUS

FRIARS, DEVILS, ATTENDANTS

Doctor Faustus

Enter Chorus.

CHORUS: Not marching now in fields of
Thrasymene*
Where Mars did mate the Carthaginians,
Nor sporting in the dalliance of love
In courts of kings where state is overturned,
Nor in the pomp of proud audacious deeds
Intends our Muse to vaunt his heavenly verse:
Only this, Gentlemen, we must perform,
The form of Faustus' fortunes good or bad.
Now is he born, his parents base of stock,
In Germany within a town called Rhodes;
Of riper years to Wittenberg he went
So soon he profits in divinity,
The fruitful plot of scholarism† graced,
That shortly he was graced with Doctor's name,
Excelling all whose sweet delight disputes
In heavenly matters of theology,
Till swollen with cunning, of a self-conceit,
His waxen wings did mount above his reach
And melting heavens conspired his overthrow.
For, falling to a devilish exercise,
He surfeits upon cursed necromancy.‡
Nothing so sweet as magic is to him,
Which he prefers before his chiefest bliss—
And this the man that in his study sits. *(exit)*

---

*Thrasymene: where Hannibal defeated the Romans in 217
†scholarism: scholarship
‡necromancy: magic; communication with the dead

13

SCENE 1

Enter Faustus in his study.

FAUSTUS: Settle thy studies, Faustus, and begin
To sound the depth of that thou wilt profess.
Having commenced, be a divine in show,
Yet level at the end of every art
And live and die in Aristotle's works:
Sweet Analytics, 'tis thou hast ravished me!
(reads)

Bene disserere est finis logicis—*
Is to dispute well logic's chiefest end?
Affords this art no greater miracle?
Then read no more; thou hast attained the end.
A greater subject fitteth Faustus' wit:
Bid philosophy farewell, now Galen come.
Be a physician, Faustus, heap up gold
And be eternized† for some wondrous cure.
(reads)

Summum bonum medicinae sanitas—
The end of physic is our bodies' health:
Why, Faustus, hast thou not attained that end?
Is not thy common talk sound aphorisms?‡
Are not thy bills§ hung up as monuments,
Whereby whole cities have escaped the plague
And thousand desperate maladies been eased?

*Bene disserere est finis logicis: translated in the next line
†eternized: made eternally famous
‡aphorisms: medical rules
§bills: prescriptions

Yet art thou still but Faustus, and a man.
Couldst thou make men to live eternally
Or, being dead, raise them to life again,
Then this profession were to be esteemed.
Physic, farewell. To the law I'll turn. *(reads)*
Si una eademque res legatur duobus,
*Alter rem, alter valorem rei, etc.—**
A pretty case of paltry legacies!
Exhaereditare filium non potest pater nisi—
A father cannot disinherit his son unless—
Such is the subject of the Institute
And universal body of the law.
His study fits a mercenary drudge
Who aims at nothing but external trash,
Too servile and illiberal for me.
When all is done, divinity is best.
Jerome's Bible, Faustus, view it well: *(reads)*
Stipendium peccati mors est—Ha!
The reward of sin is death. That's hard.
Si pecasse negamus, fallimur, et nulla est in nobis
veritas—
If we say that we have no sin
We deceive ourselves, and there's no truth in us.
Why then belike
We must sin and so consequently die,
Ay, we must die an everlasting death.
What doctrine call you this, *Che sera, sera:*
What will be, shall be? Divinity, adieu!
These metaphysics of magicians
And necromantic books are heavenly:
Lines, circles, signs, letters and characters—
Ay, these are those that Faustus most desires.
O what a world of profit and delight,

Si una eademque res legatur duobus, Alter rem, alter valorem rei: if the
same thing is bequeathed to two persons, one shall have the thing
itself, the other shall have the value of the thing

Of power, of honor, of omnipotence,
Is promised to the studious artisan!
All things that move between the quiet poles
Shall be at my command. Emperors and kings
Are but obeyed in their several provinces,
Nor can they raise the wind or rend the clouds;
But his dominion that exceeds in this
Stretcheth as far as doth the mind of man.
A sound magician is a mighty god:
Here, Faustus, try thy brains to gain a deity!
(enter Wagner)

Wagner, commend me to my dearest friends,
The German Valdes and Cornelius;
Request them earnestly to visit me.

WAGNER: I will, sir. *(exit)*

FAUSTUS: Their conference will be a greater help to me
Than all my labors, plod I ne'er so fast.

(enter the Good Angel and the Evil Angel)

GOOD ANGEL: O Faustus, lay that damned book aside
And gaze not on it, lest it tempt thy soul
And heap God's heavy wrath upon thy head.
Read, read the Scriptures! That is blasphemy.

EVIL ANGEL: Go forward, Faustus, in that famous art
Wherein all nature's treasury is contained:
Be thou on earth, as Jove is in the sky,
Lord and commander of these elements. *(exit Angels)*

FAUSTUS: How am I glutted with conceit of this!
Shall I make spirits fetch me what I please,
Resolve me of all ambiguities,
Perform what desperate enterprise I will?

I'll have them fly to India for gold,
Ransack the ocean for orient pearl,
And search all corners of the new-found world
For pleasant fruits and princely delicates;
I'll have them read me strange philosophy
And tell the secrets of all foreign kings;
I'll have them wall all Germany with brass
And make swift Rhine circle fair Wittenberg;
I'll levy soldiers with the coin they bring,
And reign sole king of all our provinces. *(enter Valdes and Cornelius)*

Valdes, sweet Valdes and Cornelius,
Know that your words have won me at the last
To practice magic and concealed arts;
Yet not your words only, but mine own fantasy,
That will receive no object for my head
But ruminates on necromantic skill.
Philosophy is odious and obscure;
Both law and physic are for petty wits;
Divinity is basest of the three,
Unpleasant, harsh, contemptible and vile:
'Tis magic, magic, that hath ravished me!
Then, gentle friends, aid me in this attempt.

VALDES: Faustus, these books, thy wit, and our experience,
Shall make all nations to canonize us.
As Indian Moors obey their Spanish lords,
So shall the subjects of every element
Be always serviceable to us three.

CORNELIUS: Like lions shall they guard us when we please.

VALDES: Like Almain rutters* with their horsemen's staves,

*Almain rutters: German horsemen

17

Or Lapland giants trotting by our sides.

CORNELIUS: Sometimes like women, or unwedded maids,
Shadowing more beauty in their airy brows
Than has the white breasts of the queen of love.

VALDES: From Venice shall they drag huge argosies,*
And from America the golden fleece
That yearly stuffs old Philip's† treasury,
If learned Faustus will be resolute.

FAUSTUS: Valdes, as resolute am I in this
As thou to live; therefore object it not.

CORNELIUS: The miracles that magic will perform
Will make thee vow to study nothing else.
He that is grounded in astrology,
Enriched with tongues, well seen in minerals,
Hath all the principles magic doth require.

VALDES: Then doubt not, Faustus, but to be renowned
And more frequented for this mystery
Than heretofore the Delphian oracle.

CORNELIUS: The spirits tell me they can dry the sea
And fetch the treasure of all foreign wrecks—
Ay, all the wealth that our forefathers hid
Within the massy‡ entrails of the earth.
Then tell me, Faustus, what shall we three want?

FAUSTUS: Nothing, Cornelius, O this cheers my soul!
Come, show me some demonstrations magical,
That I may conjure in some lusty grove
And have these joys in full possession.

*argosies: ships
†Philip: King Philip II of Spain
‡massy: massive

18

VALDES: Then haste thee to some solitary grove
And bear wise Bacon's and Albanus' works,
The Hebrew Psalter and New Testament.

CORNELIUS: And whatsoever else is requisite
We will inform thee ere our conference cease.
Valdes, first let him know the words of art,
And then, all other ceremonies learned,
Faustus may try his cunning by himself.

VALDES: First I'll instruct thee in the rudiments,
And then wilt thou be perfecter than I.

FAUSTUS: Then come and dine with me, and after
meat
We'll canvas every quiddity* thereof;
For ere I sleep I'll try what I can do:
This night I'll conjure though I die therefore.
(exit)

*quiddity: petty argument

SCENE 2

Enter three Scholars.

1ST SCHOLAR: I wonder what's become of Faustus, that was wont to make our schools ring with *sic probo?*

3RD SCHOLAR: I have the proof.

2ND AND 3RD SCHOLARS: *(together)* I have the proof.

2ND SCHOLAR: A good man.

3RD SCHOLAR: Aye.

2ND SCHOLAR: And infinite learned.

1ST SCHOLAR: But yet I wonder what's become of him.

2ND SCHOLAR: That shall we know, for see here comes his boy.

(enter Wagner carrying wine)

1ST SCHOLAR: How now, sirrah; where's thy master?

WAGNER: God in heaven knows.

2ND SCHOLAR: Why, dost not thou know?

WAGNER: Yes, I know; but it follows not that God in heaven knows.

1ST SCHOLAR: Go to, sirrah; leave your jesting and tell us where he is.

WAGNER: How now. You call yourselves scholars, yet you know not the logic of necessity. I tell thee

IT FOLLOWS NOT. Therefore acknowledge your error and be attentive.

3RD SCHOLAR: *Sic probo.* I have the proof.

2ND SCHOLAR: Didst thou not say thou knewest?

3RD SCHOLAR: Yes, sirrah, I heard you.

2ND SCHOLAR: Well, will you not tell us?

WAGNER: Yes, sir, I will tell you. Yet if you were not dunces you would never ask me such a question, for is not Faustus *corpus naturale,* and is not that *mobile?* Then wherefore should you ask me such a question?

1ST SCHOLAR: Is Faustus not within?

WAGNER: It were not for you to come within forty foot of the place of execution, although I do not doubt to see you all hanged the next sessions. Thus having triumphed over you, I will set my countenance like a puritan, and begin to speak thus: Truly, my dear brethren, my master is within at dinner with Valdes and Cornelius.

2ND SCHOLAR: God forbid—if that be so.

1ST SCHOLAR: *(overlaps)* Valdes and Cornelius!

WAGNER: As this wine, if it could speak, it would inform your worships.

3RD SCHOLAR: Wherefore are *they* come hither?

WAGNER: And so the Lord bless you, preserve you, and keep you, my dear brethren, my dear brethren. *(exit)*

1ST SCHOLAR: Valdes and Cornelius!

3RD SCHOLAR: Wherefore are they come?!

1ST SCHOLAR: Nay, then I fear he is fallen into that damned art for which they two are infamous through the world.

3RD SCHOLAR: The magic of the damned.

2ND SCHOLAR: Were he a stranger and not allied to me, yet should I grieve for him. But come, let us go and inform the Rector, and see if he by his grave counsel can reclaim him.

1ST SCHOLAR: O but I fear me nothing can reclaim him.

ALL: Nothing. *(exit)*

SCENE 3

Enter Faustus to conjure.

FAUSTUS: Now that the gloomy shadow of the earth,
Leaps from the antarctic world unto the sky
And dims the welkin with her pitchy breath,
Faustus, begin thine incantations,
And try if devils will obey thy hest,
Seeing thou has prayed and sacrificed to them.
(he draws a circle on the ground)
Within this circle is Jehovah's name
Forward and backward anagrammatized,*
The 'breviated names of holy saints,
By which the spirits are enforced to rise.
Then fear not, Faustus, but be resolute,
And try the uttermost magic can perform.
   (thunder)
Let the gods of hell look favorably upon me. Let
the triple divinity of Jehovah prevail. Spirits of
fire, air, and water, all hail Belzebub, prince of
the East, king of the fires of hell, and, Demo-
gorgon, we sacrifice to you so that Mephistophilis may rise up and appear! *(Faustus pauses;
thunder still)* Why do you delay? By Jehovah, by
Gehenna, and by the holy water which I now
sprinkle, and by the sign of the cross which I
now make, and by our prayers, now summoned

---

*anagrammatized: Faustus has written the name of God in the
pattern of a cross

23

by us, Mephistophilis, arise!

(enter a Devil)

I charge thee to return and change thy shape;
Thou art too ugly to attend on me.
Go, and return an old Franciscan friar;
That holy shape becomes a devil best.

(exit Devil)

I see there's virtue in my heavenly words:
Who would not be proficient in this art?
How pliant is this Mephistophilis,
Full of obedience and humility!
Such is the force of magic and my spells.
Now, Faustus, thou art conjuror laureate
That canst command great Mephistophilis:
Veni, veni, Mephistophile!

(enter Mephistophilis, like a Friar)

MEPH: Now, Faustus, what wouldst thou have me
do?

FAUSTUS: I charge thee wait upon me whilst I live
To do whatever Faustus shall command,
Be it to make the moon drop from her sphere
Or the ocean to overwhelm the world.

MEPH: I am a servant to great Lucifer
And may not follow thee without his leave:
No more than he commands must we perform.

FAUSTUS: Did not he charge thee to appear to me?

MEPH: No, I came now hither of mine own accord.

FAUSTUS: Did not my conjuring speeches raise thee?
Speak!

MEPH: That was the cause, but yet by accident,
For when we hear one rack the name of God,
Abjure the Scriptures and his Savior Christ,

24

We fly in hope to get his glorious soul;
Nor will we come unless he use such means
Whereby he is in danger to be damned;
Therefore the shortest cut for conjuring
Is stoutly to abjure the Trinity
And pray devoutly to the prince of hell.

FAUSTUS: So Faustus hath
Already done, and holds this principle,
There is no chief but only Belzebub,
To whom Faustus doth dedicate himself.
This word damnation terrifies not him,
For he confounds hell in Elysium;
His ghost be with the old philosophers!
But leaving these vain trifles of men's souls—
Tell me what is that Lucifer thy lord?

MEPH: Arch-regent and commander of all spirits.

FAUSTUS: Was not that Lucifer an angel once?

MEPH: Yes, Faustus, and most dearly loved of God.

FAUSTUS: How comes it, then, that he is prince of devils?

MEPH: O by aspiring pride and insolence
For which God threw him from the face of heaven.

FAUSTUS: And what are you that live with Lucifer?

MEPH: Unhappy spirits that fell with Lucifer,
Conspired against our God with Lucifer,
And are forever damned with Lucifer.

FAUSTUS: Where are you damned?

MEPH: In hell.

FAUSTUS: How comes it, then, that thou art out of hell?

MEPH: Why, this is hell, nor am I out of it:

Thinkst thou that I who saw the face of God
And tasted the eternal joys of heaven
Am not tormented with ten thousand hells
In being deprived of everlasting bliss?
O Faustus, leave these frivolous demands
Which strike a terror to my fainting soul!

FAUSTUS: What, is great Mephistophilis so
passionate
For being deprived of the joys of heaven?
Learn thou of Faustus' manly fortitude,
And scorn those joys thou never shalt possess.
Go, bear these tidings to great Lucifer:
Seeing Faustus hath incurred eternal death
By desperate thoughts against Jove's deity,
Say he surrenders up to him his soul
So he will spare him four-and-twenty years,
Letting him live in all voluptuousness,
Having thee ever to attend on me:
To give me whatsoever I shall ask,
To tell me whatsoever I demand,
To slay mine enemies and aid my friends,
And always be obedient to my will.
Go, and return to mighty Lucifer,
And meet me in my study at midnight
And then resolve me of thy master's mind.

MEPH: I will, Faustus. *(exit)*

FAUSTUS: Had I as many souls as there be stars
I'd give them all for Mephistophilis!
By him I'll be great emperor of the world,
And make a bridge through the moving air
To pass the ocean with a band of men;
I'll join the hills that bind the Afric shore
And make that country continent to Spain,
And both contributory to my crown;
The Emperor shall not live but by my leave,
Nor any potentate of Germany.

Now that I have obtained what I desire
I'll live in speculation of this art
Till Mephistophilis return again. *(exit)*

SCENE 4

Enter Wagner and the Clown.

WAGNER: Sirrah, boy, come hither.

CLOWN: How, boy? Swounds, boy! I hope you have seen many boys with such beards as I have. Boy, quotha!

WAGNER: Tell me then, sirrah, wilt thou serve me? Wilt thou wait upon me whilst I live?—Hast thou any comings in?

CLOWN: Ay, and goings out, too.

WAGNER: Alas, poor slave. See how poverty jests in his nakedness: the villain is bare and out of service, and so hungry that I know he would give his soul to the Devil for a shoulder of mutton, though it were blood-raw.

CLOWN: How, my soul to the Devil for a shoulder of mutton, though it were blood-raw? Not so, good friend: by'r Lady, I had need have it well roasted, and good sauce to it, if I pay so dear. My soul to the Devil quotha!

WAGNER: Well, wilt thou serve me and bind yourself presently unto me for seven years?

CLOWN: Seven years! quotha.

WAGNER: If thou deny, I'll turn all the lice about

thee into devils familiar, and they shall tear thee in pieces.

CLOWN: You may save that labor; they are too familiar with me already. Swounds, they are as bold with my flesh as if they had paid for my meat and drink.

WAGNER: Hold, take these guilders. *(gives money)*

CLOWN: And what should I do with these?

WAGNER: Why now, sirrah, thou art at an hour's warning whensoever or wheresoever the Devil shall fetch thee.

CLOWN: No, no! Here, take your gridirons again.

WAGNER: Truly, I'll none of them.

CLOWN: Truly, but you shall.

WAGNER: Bear witness, I gave them him.

CLOWN: Bear witness, I give them you again.

WAGNER: Well, I will cause two devils presently to fetch thee away. Baliol and Belcher! *(conjures)*

CLOWN: Let your Belly-oh and your Belcher come here. I'll belch them and I'll knock them, they were never so knocked since they were devils.

(enter two Devils, and the Clown runs up and down crying)

WAGNER: How now, sirrah, wilt thou serve me now?

CLOWN: Yes, good Wagner, take away your devils!

WAGNER: Baliol and Belcher! Spirits away! *(exit Devils)*

CLOWN: What, are they gone? A vengeance on them, they have vile long nails! There was a he-devil and a she-devil. I'll tell you how you shall know them: all he-devils has horns, and all she-devils has clefts.

WAGNER: Now, sirrah, wilt thou follow me and wait upon me while I live?

CLOWN: If I should serve you, would you teach me to raise up Banios and Belcheos?

WAGNER: I will teach thee to turn thyself to anything—to a dog, or a cat, or a mouse, or a rat, or anything.

CLOWN: How? A Christian fellow to a dog or a cat, a mouse or a rat? No, no, sir! If you turn me into anything, let it be in the likeness of a little pretty frisking flea, that I may be here and there and everywhere. O I'll tickle the pretty wenches' plackets, I'll be amongst them, i'faith!

WAGNER: Well, sirrah, come.

CLOWN: But do you hear, Wagner?

WAGNER: How? Baliol and Belcher!

CLOWN: O Lord, I pray sir, let Banio and Belcher go sleep.

WAGNER: Villain, call me Master Wagner, and let thy left eye be diametrally fixt upon my right heel with *quasi vestigias nostras insistere. (exits)*

CLOWN: God forgive me, he speaks Dutch fustian. Well, I'll follow him, I'll serve him; that's flat. *(exits)*

SCENE 5

Enter Faustus in his study.

FAUSTUS: Now, Faustus, must thou needs be damn-
ed
And canst thou not be saved.
What boots it, then, to think of God or heaven?
Away with such vain fancies, and despair—
Despair in God and trust in Belzebub.
Now go not backward, no!
Faustus, be resolute: why waverest thou?
O something soundeth in mine ears:
"Abjure this magic, turn to God again!"
Ay, and Faustus will turn to God again.
To God? He loves thee not;
The God thou servest is thine own appetite,
Wherein is fixed the love of Belzebub.
To him I'll build an altar and a church
And offer lukewarm blood of newborn babes.

(enter Good Angel and Evil Angel)

GOOD ANGEL: Sweet Faustus, leave that execrable
art.

EVIL ANGEL: Go forward, Faustus, in that famous
art.

FAUSTUS: Contrition, prayer, repentance—what of
them?

GOOD ANGEL: O they are means to bring thee unto
heaven!

EVIL ANGEL: Rather illusions, fruits of lunacy,
That makes men foolish that do trust them
most.

GOOD ANGEL: Sweet Faustus, think of heaven and
heavenly things.

EVIL ANGEL: No, Faustus, think of honor and of
wealth. *(exit Angels)*

FAUSTUS: Of wealth!
Why, the seigniory of Emden shall be mine.
When Mephistophilis shall stand by me
What God can hurt me? Faustus, thou art safe;
Cast no more doubts. Come, Mephistophilis,
And bring glad tidings from great Lucifer.
Is't not midnight? Come, Mephistophilis!
  Veni, veni, Mephistophile!

(enter Mephistophilis)

Now tell me what says Lucifer, thy lord?

MEPH: That I shall wait on Faustus whilst he lives,
So he will buy my service with his soul.

FAUSTUS: Already Faustus hath hazarded that for
thee.

MEPH: But, Faustus, thou must bequeath it sol-
emnly
And write a deed of gift with thine own blood,
For that security craves great Lucifer.
If thou deny it, I will back to hell.

FAUSTUS: Stay, Mephistophilis, and tell me, what
good
Will my soul do thy lord?

MEPH: Enlarge his kingdom.

FAUSTUS: Is that the reason why he tempts us thus?

MEPH: Misery loveth company.

FAUSTUS: Why, have you any pain that tortures others?

MEPH: As great as have the human souls of men.
But tell me, Faustus, shall I have thy soul?
And I will be thy slave, and wait on thee,
And tell thee more than thou hast wit to ask.

FAUSTUS: Ay, Mephistophilis, I give it thee.

MEPH: Then, Faustus, stab thine arm courageously,
And bind thy soul that at some certain day
Great Lucifer may claim it as his own,
And then be thou as great as Lucifer.

FAUSTUS: Lo, Mephistophilis, for love of thee *(stabbing his arm)*
I cut mine arm, and with my proper blood
Assure my soul to be great Lucifer's.
Chief lord and regent of perpetual night,
View here the blood that trickles from mine arm
And let it be propitious for my wish!

MEPH: But, Faustus, thou must
Write it in manner of a deed of gift.

FAUSTUS: Ay, so I will. *(writes)* But Mephistophilis,
My blood congeals and I can write no more.

MEPH: I'll fetch thee fire to dissolve it straight.
(exit)

FAUST: What might the staying of my blood portend?
Is it unwilling I should write this bill?
Why streams it not, that I may write afresh?
"Faustus gives to thee his soul"—ah, there it stayed.
Why shouldst thou not? Is not thy soul thine own?

33

Then write again: "Faustus gives to thee his soul."

(reenter Mephistophilis with a chafer of coals)

MEPH: Here's fire; come, Faustus, set it on.

FAUSTUS: So: now the blood begins to clear again;
Now will I make an end immediately. *(writes)*

MEPH: *(aside)* O what will not I do to obtain his soul!

FAUSTUS: It is finished—this bill is ended,
And Faustus hath bequeathed his soul to Lucifer.
But what is this inscription on mine arm?
"Flee, man!" Whither should I fly?
If unto God, he'll throw me down to hell.
My senses are deceived; here's nothing writ.
I see it plain: here in this place is writ
"Flee, man!" Yet shall not Faustus fly.

MEPH: I'll fetch him somewhat to delight his mind. *(exits)*

(reenter Mephistophilis with Devils, giving crowns and rich apparel to Faustus, and dance, and then depart)

FAUSTUS: Speak, Mephistophilis, what means this show?

MEPH: Nothing, Faustus, but to delight thy mind withal
And to show thee what magic can perform.

FAUSTUS: But may I raise up spirits when I please?

MEPH: Ay, Faustus, and do greater things than these.

FAUSTUS: Then there's enough for a thousand souls.

Here, Mephistophilis, receive this scroll,
A deed of gift of body and of soul;
But yet conditionally that thou perform
All articles prescribed between us both.

MEPH: Faustus, I swear by hell and Lucifer
To effect all promises between us made.

FAUSTUS: Then hear me read them: *(reads)*
"On these conditions following:
First, that Faustus may be a spirit in form and
  substance.
Secondly, that Mephistophilis shall be his
  servant and at his command.
Thirdly, that Mephistophilis shall do for him,
  and bring him whatsoever he desireth.
Fourthly, that he shall be in his chamber or
  house invisible.
Lastly, that he shall appear to the said John
  Faustus at all times, in what form or shape
  soever he please.
I, John Faustus of Wittenberg, Doctor, do give
body and soul to Lucifer, Prince of the East,
and his minister Mephistophilis, and further-
more grant unto them, that twenty-four years
being expired, the articles above written yet
unbroken, full power to carry the said John
Faustus body and soul, flesh, blood, or goods,
into their habitation wheresoever.
By me John Faustus."

MEPH: Speak, Faustus, do you deliver this as your
deed?

FAUSTUS: Ay, take it, and the Devil give thee good
on't.

MEPH: Now, Faustus, ask what thou wilt.

FAUSTUS: First will I question with thee about hell.
Tell me, where is the place that men call hell?

MEPH: Under the heavens.

FAUSTUS: Ay, but whereabout?

MEPH: Within the bowels of these elements,
Where we are tortured and remain forever.
Hell hath no limits, nor is circumscribed
In one self place, for where we are is hell,
And where hell is there must we ever be;
And, to conclude, when all the world dissolves,
And every creature shall be purified,
All places shall be hell that is not heaven.

FAUSTUS: Come, I think hell's a fable.

MEPH: Ay, think so, till experience change thy
mind.

FAUSTUS: Why, thinkst thou then that Faustus shall
be damned?

MEPH: Ay, of necessity, for here's the scroll
Wherein thou hast given thy soul to Lucifer.

FAUSTUS: Ay, and body too; but what of that?
Thinkst thou that Faustus is so fond to imagine
That after this life there is any pain?
Tush, these are trifles and mere old wives' tales.

MEPH: But, Faustus, I am an instance to prove the
contrary,
For I am damned, and am now in hell.

FAUSTUS: How, now in hell?
Nay, and this be hell I'll willingly be damned
here.
What, walking, disputing, et cetera?
But leaving off this, let me have a wife,
The fairest maid in Germany,
For I am wanton and lascivious
And cannot live without a wife.

36

MEPH: How, a wife?
I prithee, Faustus, talk not of a wife.

FAUSTUS: Nay, sweet Mephistophilis, fetch me one,
for I will have one.

MEPH: Well, thou wilt have one. Sit there till I
come;
I'll fetch thee a wife in the Devil's name. *(exit)*

*(reenter Mephistophilis with a Devil dressed like a
woman, with fireworks)*

MEPH: Tell me, Faustus, how dost thou like thy
wife?

FAUSTUS: A plague on her for a hot whore! *(exit
Devil)*

MEPH: Tut, Faustus,
Marriage is but a ceremonial toy.
If thou lovest me, think no more of it.
I'll cull thee out the fairest courtesans
And bring them every morning to thy bed;
She whom thine eye shall like thy heart shall
have,
Be she as chaste as was Penelope,
As wise as Saba, or as beautiful
As was bright Lucifer before his fall.
Hold, take this book: peruse it thoroughly.
The iterating of these lines brings gold,
The framing of this circle on the ground
Brings whirlwinds, tempests, thunder and
lightning;
Pronounce this thrice devoutly to thyself
And men in armor shall appear to thee,
Ready to execute what thou desirest.

FAUSTUS: My thanks, Mephistophilis, yet fain would
I have a book wherein I might behold all spells

37

and incantations, that I might raise up spirits when I please.

MEPH: Here they are in this book. *(turn to them)*

FAUSTUS: Now would I have a book where I might see all characters and planets of the heavens, that I might know their motions and dispositions.

MEPH: Here they are too. *(turn to them)*

FAUSTUS: Nay, let me have one book more, and then I have done, wherein I might see all plants, herbs, and trees that grow upon the earth.

MEPH: Here they be.

FAUSTUS: O thou art deceived!

MEPH: Tut, I warrant thee. *(turn to them)*

(they exit)

SCENE 6

Enter Faustus in his study, and Mephistophilis.

FAUSTUS: When I behold the heavens, then I repent
And curse thee, wicked Mephistophilis,
Because thou hast deprived me of those joys.

MEPH: Why, Faustus,
Thinkst thou heaven is such a glorious thing?
I tell thee, 'tis not half so fair as thou,
Or any man that breathes on earth.

FAUSTUS: How provest thou that?

MEPH: It was made for man; therefore is man
more excellent.

FAUSTUS: If it were made for man 'twas made for
me.
I will renounce this magic and repent.

(enter Good Angel and Evil Angel)

GOOD ANGEL: Faustus, repent; yet God will pity
thee.

EVIL ANGEL: Thou art a spirit; God cannot pity
thee.

FAUSTUS: Who buzzeth in mine ears I am a spirit?
Be I a devil yet God may pity me.
Ay, God will pity me if I repent.

EVIL ANGEL: Ay, but Faustus never shall repent. *(exit
Angels)*

39

FAUSTUS: My heart's so hardened I cannot repent.
Scarce can I name salvation, faith, or heaven,
But fearful echoes thunder in mine ears:
"Faustus, thou art damned!" Then swords and
knives,
Poison, guns, halters, and envenomed steel
Are laid before me to dispatch myself,
And long ere this I should have slain myself
Had not sweet pleasure conquered deep
despair.
Have I not made blind Homer sing to me
Of Alexander's* love and Oenon's death,
And hath not he that built the walls of Thebes
With ravishing sound of his melodious harp
Made music with my Mephistophilis?
Why should I die, then, or basely despair?
I am resolved Faustus shall ne'er repent.
Come, Mephistophilis, let us dispute again
And argue of divine astrology.
Tell me, are there many heavens above the
moon?
Are all celestial bodies but one globe,
As is the substance of this centric earth?

MEPH: As are the elements, such are the spheres,
Mutually folded in each other's orb;
Nor are the names of Saturn, Mars, or Jupiter
Feigned, but are erring stars.

FAUSTUS: But tell me, have they all one motion,
both *situ et tempore?*†

MEPH: All jointly move from East to West in
twenty-four hours upon the poles of the world,
but differ in their motion upon the poles of the
zodiac.

*Alexander: Paris, once the lover of Oenone
†*situ et tempore:* in place and time

FAUSTUS: Tush, these slender trifles Wagner can decide.
Hath Mephistophilis no greater skill?
Who knows not the double motion of the planets?
The first is finished in a natural day;
The second thus, as Saturn in thirty years, Jupiter in twelve, Mars in four, the Sun, Venus, and Mercury in a year, the Moon in twenty-eight days. Tush, these are freshmen's suppositions. But tell me, hath every sphere a dominion or *Intelligentia*?

MEPH: Ay.

FAUSTUS: How many heavens or spheres are there?

MEPH: Nine: the seven planets, the firmament, and the empyreal heaven.

FAUSTUS: But is there not *coelum igneum, et crystallinum*?*

MEPH: No, Faustus, they be but fables.

FAUSTUS: Well, resolve me in this question: why have we not conjunctions, oppositions, aspects, eclipses,† all at one time, but in some years we have more, in some less?

MEPH: Because of the unequal motion in relation to the whole.

FAUSTUS: Well, I am answered. Tell me, who made the world?

MEPH: I will not.

---

coelum igneum, et crystallinum: a burning heaven and a crystalline heaven
†conjunctions, oppositions, etc.: astrological terms for the positions of the planets

FAUSTUS: Sweet Mephistophilis, tell me.

MEPH: Move me not, for I will not tell thee.

FAUSTUS: Villain, have I not bound thee to tell me anything?

MEPH: Ay, that is not against our kingdom; but this is.
Think thou on hell, Faustus, for thou art damned.

FAUSTUS: Think, Faustus, upon God that made the world!

MEPH: Remember this! *(exit)*

FAUSTUS: Ay, go, accursed spirit, to ugly hell;
'Tis thou has damned distressed Faustus' soul.
Is't not too late?

(enter Good Angel and Evil Angel)

EVIL ANGEL: Too late.

GOOD ANGEL: Never too late, if Faustus can repent.

EVIL ANGEL: If thou repent, devils shall tear thee in pieces.

GOOD ANGEL: Repent, and they shall never raze thy skin. *(exit Angels)*

FAUSTUS: Ah Christ, my Savior!
Seek to save distressed Faustus' soul.

(enter Lucifer, Belzebub, and Mephistophilis)

LUCIFER: Christ cannot save thy soul, for he is just;
There's none but have interest in the same.

FAUSTUS: O who art thou that lookst so terrible?

LUCIFER: I am Lucifer.

FAUSTUS: O Faustus, they are come to fetch away thy soul!

LUCIFER: We come to tell thee thou dost injure us: Thou callst on Christ, contrary to thy promise. Thou shouldst not think of God; think of the Devil,—

FAUSTUS: Nor will I henceforth. Pardon me in this,
And Faustus vows never to look to heaven,
Never to name God or to pray to him,
To burn his Scriptures, slay his ministers,
And make my spirits pull his churches down.

LUCIFER: Do so, and we will highly gratify thee. Faustus, we are come from hell to show thee some pastime: sit down, and thou shalt see all the Seven Deadly Sins appear in their proper shapes.

FAUSTUS: That sight will be as pleasing unto me as paradise was to Adam, the first day of his creation.

LUCIFER: Talk not of paradise nor creation, but mark this show; talk of the Devil and nothing else. Come, away!

(enter the Seven Deadly Sins)

Now, Faustus, examine them of their several names and dispositions.

FAUSTUS: What are thou, the first?

PRIDE: I am Pride. I disdain to have any parents, nor Eve, nor Adam. I am like to Ovid's flea: I can creep into every corner of a wench; sometimes like a periwig I sit upon her brow; next like a necklace I hang about her neck, or like a fan of feathers I kiss her lips; and do what I list. But fie, what a stench is here! I'll not speak

43

another word except the ground were perfumed and covered with a golden cloth.

FAUSTUS: Thou art a proud knave indeed. What art thou, the second?

COVETOUSNESS: I am Covetousness, begotten of an old miser in an old leathern bag; and, might I have my wish, I would desire that this house and all the people in it were turned to gold, that I might lock you up in my chest. O my sweet gold!

FAUSTUS: What art thou, the third?

WRATH: I am Wrath. I had neither father nor mother; I leaped out of a lion's mouth when I was scarce half an hour old, and ever since I have run up and down the world with this case of rapiers; wounding myself when I had nobody to fight withal. I was born in hell; and look to it, for some of you shall be my father.

FAUSTUS: What art thou, the fourth?

ENVY: I am Envy, begotten of a chimney-sweeper and an oyster-wife. I cannot read, and therefore wish all books were burned. I am lean with seeing others eat. O that there would come a famine through all the world, that all might die, and I live alone; then thou shouldst see how fat I would be! But must thou sit and I stand? Come down, with a vengeance!

FAUSTUS: Away, envious rascal! What art thou, the fifth?

GLUTTONY: Who, I sir? I am Gluttony. My parents are all dead, and the devil on it, they have left me but a bare pension, but thirty meals a day and ten quarts of ale—a small trifle to suffice nature. O I come of a royal parentage: my grandfather was a gammon of bacon, my grandmother a hogshead of claret wine. My godfathers were these: Peter Pickle-herring and Martin Micklemas-beef. O but my godmother— she was a jolly gentlewoman: her name was mistress Margery March-beer. Now, Faustus, thou hast heard all my forebears; wilt thou bid me to supper?

FAUSTUS: No, I'll see thee hanged! Thou wilt eat up all my victuals.

GLUTTONY: Then the Devil choke thee.

FAUSTUS: Choke thyself, glutton. What art thou, the sixth?

SLOTH: I am Sloth. I was begotten on a sunny bank, where I have lain ever since, and you have done me great injury to bring me from thence; let me be carried thither again by Gluttony and Lechery. I'll not speak another word for a king's ransom.

FAUSTUS: What are you, mistress minx, the seventh and last?

LECHERY: Who, I, sir? I am one that loves an inch of raw mutton or the cod from thy cod piece, and the first letter of my name begins with L—echery.

LUCIFER: Away, to hell, to hell! *(exit the sins)* Now, Faustus, how dost thou like this?

FAUSTUS: O this feeds my soul!

LUCIFER: Tut, Faustus, in hell is all manner of delight.

FAUSTUS: O that I might see hell and return again, how happy were I then!

45

LUCIFER: Thou shalt. I will send for thee at midnight. In mean time take this book, peruse it thoroughly, and thou shalt turn thyself into what shape thou wilt.

FAUSTUS: Great thanks, mighty Lucifer;
This will I keep as chary as my life.

LUCIFER: Farewell, Faustus, and think on the Devil.

FAUSTUS: Farewell, great Lucifer. Come, Mephistophilis. *(exit all)*

INTERMISSION

SCENE 7

Enter Wagner alone, as Chorus.

WAGNER: Learned Faustus,
To know the secrets of astronomy
Graven in the book of Jove's high firmament,
Did mount himself to scale Olympus' top,
Being seated in a chariot burning bright
Drawn by the strength of yokcd dragons' necks:
He now is gone to prove cosmography,
And, as I guess, will first arrive at Rome
To see the Pope and manner of his court,
And take some part of holy Peter's feast,
The which this day is highly solemnized. *(exit Wagner)*

(enter Faustus and Mephistophilis)

FAUSTUS: Having now, my good Mephistophilis,
Passed with delight the stately town of Trier
Environed round with airy mountain tops,
From Paris next coasting the realm of France,
We saw the river Main fall into Rhine,
Whose banks are set with groves of fruitful
vines;
Then up to Naples, rich Campagna,
Whose buildings fair and gorgeous to the eye,
The streets straight forth and paved with finest
brick
Quarters the town in four equivalents.
There saw we learned Virgil's golden tomb,

47

The way he cut, an English mile in length,
Through a rock of stone in one night's space.
From thence to Venice, Padua, and the rest,
In midst of which a sumptuous temple stands
That threats the stars with her aspiring top.
Thus hitherto hath Faustus spent his time.
But tell me now, what resting place is this?
Hast thou, as erst I did command,
Conducted me within the walls of Rome?

MEPH: Faustus, I have; and because we will not be
unprovided, I have taken up his Holiness' privy
chamber for our use.

FAUSTUS: I hope his Holiness will bid us welcome.

MEPH: Tut, 'tis no matter, man; we'll be bold with
his good venison.
And now, my Faustus, that thou mayst perceive
What Rome containeth to delight thee with,
Know that this city stands upon seven hills
Just through the midst runs flowing Tiber's
stream,
With winding banks that cut it in two parts,
Over the which four stately bridges lean
That makes safe passage to each part of Rome.
Besides the gates and high pyramides
Which Julius Caesar brought from Africa.

FAUSTUS: Now by the kingdoms of infernal rule,
Of Styx, Acheron, and the fiery lake
Of ever-burning Phlegethon, I swear
That I do long to see the monuments
And situation of bright-splendent Rome.
Come, therefore, let's away.

MEPH: Nay, Faustus, stay; I know you'd fain see
the Pope
And take some part of holy Peter's feast,

48

Where thou shalt see a troop of bald-pate friars
Whose *summum bonum* is in belly-cheer.

FAUSTUS: Well, I am content to compass then some
sport
Whilst I am here on Earth let me be cloyed
With all things that delight the heart of man.
My four and twenty years of liberty
I'll spend in pleasure and in dalliance
That Faustus' name while this bright frame
   doth stand
May be admired through the furthest land.
Is not all power on earth bestowed on us?
And therefore though we would we cannot err.
Then charm me that I may be invisible,
To do what I please
Unseen of any whilst I stay in Rome.

(Mephistophilis gestures)

MEPH: So, Faustus; now
Do what thou wilt thou shalt not be discerned.

*(Sound a sennet. Enter the Pope and the Cardinal of
Lorraine to the banquet, with Friars attending.)*

POPE: Cast down our footstool!

CARDINAL: *(to Friar)* Stoop! Whilst on thy back his
Holiness ascends Saint Peter's chair.

POPE: Sound trumpets then, for thus Saint Peter's
heir upon thy back ascends Saint Peter's chair.

POPE: My Lord of Lorraine, will't please you draw
near?

FAUSTUS: Fall to, and the Devil choke you and you
spare.

POPE: How now, who's that which spake? Friars
look about.

FRIAR: Here's nobody, if it like your Holiness.

POPE: My lord, here is a dainty dish was sent me from the Bishop of Milan.

FAUSTUS: I thank you, sir. *(snatches it)*

POPE: How now, who's that which snatched the meat from me? Will no man look? My lord, this dish was sent me from the Cardinal of Florence.

FAUSTUS: You say true; I'll have that too. *(snatches it)*

POPE: What, again! My lord, I'll drink to your grace.

FAUSTUS: I'll pledge your grace. *(snatches it)*

CARDINAL: My Lord, it may be some ghost newly crept out of Purgatory come to beg a pardon of your Holiness.

POPE: It may be so. Friars, prepare a dirge to lay the fury of this ghost. Once again, my lord, fall to. *(the Pope crosseth himself)*

FAUSTUS: What, are you crossing of yourself? Well, use that trick no more, I would advise you. *(cross again)*
Well, that's the second time. Aware the third, I give you fair warning. *(cross again, and Faustus hits him a box of the ear, and they all run away)*

POPE: Help me, my lords! Damned be this soul for ever for this deed!

FAUSTUS: Come on, Mephistophilis, what shall we do?

MEPH: Nay, I know not; we shall be cursed with bell, book, and candle.

FAUSTUS: How! bell, book, and candle, candle, book, and bell,

Forward and backward to curse Faustus to hell.
Anon you shall hear a hog grunt, a calf bleat,
    and an ass bray,
Because it is Saint Peter's holy day.

(enter all the Friars to sing the dirge)

FRIAR: Come, brethren, let's about our business
with good devotion.

(all sing)

Cursed be he that stole away his Holiness' meat
    from the table—*maledicat dominus!**
Cursed be he that struck his Holiness a blow on
    the face—*maledicat dominus!*
Cursed be he that took Friar Sandelo a blow on
    the pate—*maledicat dominus!*
Cursed be he that disturbeth our holy dirge—
    maledicat dominus!
Cursed be he that took away his Holiness' wine—
    maledicat dominus! Et omnes sancti!† Amen.

*(beat the Friars, and fling fireworks among them, and
so exit)*

---

*maledicat dominus: the Lord curse him
†*Et omnes sancti:* and all the saints

SCENE 8

Enter Chorus.

CHORUS: When Faustus had with pleasure ta'en the
view
Of rarest things and royal courts of kings,
He stayed his course and so returned home,
Where such as bear his absence but with grief,
I mean his friends and nearest companions,
Did gratulate his safety with kind words,
And in their conference of what befell
Touching his journey through the world and
air,
They put forth questions of astrology
Which Faustus answered with such learned skill
As they admired and wondered at his wit.
Now is his fame spread forth in every land:
Amongst the rest the Emperor is one,
Carolus the Fifth,* at whose palace now
Faustus is feasted mongst his noblemen.
What there he did in trial of his art
I leave untold, your eyes shall see performed.

*(enter Emperor, Empress, Faustus, Mephistophilis, and
a Knight, with attendants)*

EMPEROR: Master Doctor Faustus, I have heard
strange report of thy knowledge in the black art,
how that none can compare with thee for the

*Carolus the Fifth: Charles V, emperor of the Holy Roman Empire

rare effects of magic. They say thou hast a familiar spirit, by whom thou canst accomplish what thou list. This, therefore, is my request, that thou let me see some proof of thy skill, that mine eyes may be witnesses to confirm what mine ears have heard reported.

KNIGHT: *(aside)* I'faith, he looks much like a conjuror.

FAUSTUS: My gracious Sovereign, though I must confess myself far inferior to the report men have published, yet I am content to do whatsoever your majesty shall command me.

EMPEROR: Then, Doctor Faustus, mark what I shall say:
As I was sometime solitary set
Within my closet, sundry thoughts arose
About the honor of mine ancestors—
How they had won by prowess such exploits,
Got such riches, subdued so many kingdoms,
As we that do succeed shall,
I fear me, never attain to that degree
Amongst which kings is Alexander the Great,
Chief spectacle of the world's pre-eminence,
The bright shining of whose glorious acts
Lightens the world with his reflecting beams,
As when I hear but motion made of him
It grieves my soul I never saw the man.
If, therefore, thou by cunning of thine art
Canst raise this man from hollow vaults below
Where lies entombed this famous conqueror,
And bring him with his beauteous paramour,
Thou shalt both satisfy my just desire
And give me cause to praise thee whilst I live.

FAUSTUS: My gracious Lord, I am ready to accomplish your request, so far forth as by art and power of my spirit I am able to perform.

53

KNIGHT: *(aside)* I'faith, that's just nothing at all.

FAUSTUS: But if it like your Grace, it is not in my ability to present before your eyes the true substantial bodies of those two deceased princes which long since are consumed to dust.

KNIGHT: *(aside)* Ay marry, Master Doctor, now there's a sign of grace in you, when you will confess the truth.

FAUSTUS: But such spirits as can lively resemble Alexander and his paramour shall appear before your Grace.

EMPEROR: Go to, Master Doctor; let me see them presently.

KNIGHT: Do you hear, Master Doctor, you bring Alexander and his paramour before the Emperor?

FAUSTUS: How then, sir?

KNIGHT: I'faith, that's true as Diana turned me to a stag.

FAUSTUS: No, sir, but when Actaeon died he left the horns for you. Mephistophilis, be gone! *(exit Mephistophilis, Faustus prays)*

KNIGHT: Nay, and you go to conjuring I'll be gone. *(exit Knight)*

FAUSTUS: I'll meet with you anon for interrupting me so—
Here they are, my gracious Lord.

(enter Mephistophilis with spirits simulating Alexander and his paramour)

EMPEROR: Master Doctor, I heard this lady while she lived had a wart or mole in her neck. How shall I know whether it be so or no?

FAUSTUS: Your Highness may boldly go and see.

(Emperor sees the mole; then spirits exit)

EMPEROR: Sure these are no spirits but the true substantial bodies of those two deceased princes.

FAUSTUS: Will't please your Highness now to send for the knight that was so pleasant with me here of late?

EMPEROR: One of you call him forth.

(enter the Knight with a pair of horns on his head)

How now, sir knight! Why, I had thought thou hadst been a bachelor, but now I see thou hast a wife that not only gives thee horns but makes thee wear them. Feel on thy head.

KNIGHT: Thou damned wretch and execrable dog,
Bred in the concave of some monstrous rock,
How darest thou thus abuse a gentleman?
Villain, I say, undo what thou hast done!

FAUSTUS: O not so fast, sir.
Are you remembered how you crossed me in my conference with the Emperor? I think I have met with you for it.

EMPEROR: Good Master Doctor, at my entreaty release him; he hath done penance sufficient.

FAUSTUS: My gracious Lord, not so much for the injury he offered me here in your presence, as to delight you with some mirth hath Faustus worthily requited this injurious knight, I am content to release him of his horns. And, sir knight, hereafter speak well of scholars. Mephistophilis, transform him straight. *(exit Knight)*

EMPEROR: Believe me, Master Doctor, this merriment hath much pleased me.

55

FAUSTUS: My gracious Lord, I am glad it contents you so well. But it may be, Madam, you take no delight in this. I have heard that great-bellied women do long for some dainties or other: what is it, Madam? Tell me, and you shall have it.

EMPRESS: For I see your courteous intent to pleasure me, I will not hide from you the thing my heart desires, and were it now summer, as it is January and the dead time of the winter, I would desire no better meat than a dish of ripe grapes.

FAUSTUS: Alas, Madam, that's nothing. Mephistophilis, be gone! *(exit Mephistophilis)* Were it a greater thing than this, so it would content you you should have it.

(reenter Mephistophilis with the grapes)

Here they be, Madam: will't please you taste on them? How do you like them, Madam? be they good?

EMPRESS: Believe me, Master Doctor, they be the best grapes that e'er I tasted in my life before.

FAUSTUS: I am glad they content you so, Madam.

EMPEROR: Come, Madam, let us in,
Where you must well reward this learned man
For the great kindness he hath showed to you.
(exit)

FAUSTUS: I humbly thank your Grace.

SCENE 9

Enter Mephistophilis.

FAUSTUS: Now, Mephistophilis, the restless course
That time doth run with calm and silent foot,
Shortening my days and thread of vital life,
Calls for the payment of my latest years.
Therefore, sweet Mephistophilis, let us
Make haste to Wittenberg.
Thy fatal time doth draw to final end,
Despair doth drive distrust unto my thoughts.
Confound these passions with a quiet sleep:
Tush, Christ did call the thief upon the cross;
Then rest thee, Faustus, quiet in conceit. *(sleeps
in his chair)*

SCENE 10

Enter Clown with a book in his hand.

CLOWN: O this is admirable! Here I ha' stolen one of Doctor Faustus' conjuring books, and, i'faith, I mean to search some circles for my own use: now will I make all the maidens in our parish dance at my pleasure stark naked before me, and so by that means I shall see more than e'er I felt or saw yet.

(enter Ralph calling Clown)

RALPH: Clown, prithee come away, there's a gentleman tarries to have his horse, and he would have his things rubbed and made clean. He keeps such a chafing about it, and she has sent me to look thee out; prithee, come away.

CLOWN: Keep out, keep out, or else you are blown up, you are dismembered, Ralph; keep out, for I am about a roaring piece of work.

RALPH: Come, what doest thou with that same book? Thou canst not read.

CLOWN: Yes, my master and mistress shall find that I can read—he for his forehead, she for her private study. She's born to bear with me, or else my art fails.

RALPH: Why, Clown, what book is that?

58

CLOWN: What book? Why the most intolerable book for conjuring that e'er was invented by any brimstone devil.

RALPH: Canst thou conjure with it?

CLOWN: I can do all these things easily with it: first, I can make thee drunk with wine at any tavern in Europe for nothing. And more, Ralph, if thou hast any mind to Nan Spit our kitchen maid, then turn her and wind her to thy own use as often as thou wilt, and at midnight.

RALPH: O brave Clown! Shall I have Nan Spit, and to mine own use?

CLOWN: *(imitating Faustus)*
I am ready to accomplish your request—so far forth as by art
And power of my spirit I am able to perform.

RALPH: Go to Master Doctor, let me see her presently.

(Clown imitates Faustus in Latin prayer. Nan Spit appears from kitchen. Ralph chases her. Clown is frightened by fireworks.)

SCENE 11

Enter Wagner alone.

WAGNER: I think my master means to die shortly
For he hath given to me all his goods;
And yet methinks if that death were near
He would not banquet, and carouse, and swill
Amongst the students, as even now he doth,
Who are at supper with such belly-cheer
As Wagner ne'er beheld in all his life.
See where they come: belike the feast is ended.
(exit)

(enter Faustus and Mephistophilis with two or three Scholars)

1ST SCHOLAR: Master Doctor Faustus, since our conference about fair ladies, which was the beautifullest in all the world, we have determined with ourselves that Helen of Greece was the admirablest lady that ever lived. Therefore, Master Doctor, if you will do us that favor as to let us see that peerless dame of Greece whom all the world admires for majesty, we should think ourselves much beholding unto you.

FAUSTUS: Gentlemen,
For that I know your friendship is unfeigned,
And Faustus' custom is not to deny
The just requests of those that wish him well,
You shall behold that peerless dame of Greece,
No otherways for pomp and majesty

60

Than when Sir Paris crossed the seas with her
And brought the spoils to rich Dardania.
Be silent, then, for danger is in words.

(music sounds, and Helen passes over the stage)

2ND SCHOLAR: Too simple is my wit to tell her praise
Whom all the world admires for majesty.

3RD SCHOLAR: No marvel though the angry Greeks
pursued
With ten years' war the rape of such a queen
Whose heavenly beauty passeth all compare.

1ST SCHOLAR: Since we have seen the pride of Na-
ture's works
And only paragon of excellence,
Let us depart, and for this glorious deed
Happy and blessed be Faustus evermore.

FAUSTUS: Gentlemen, farewell; the same I wish to
you. *(Scholars exit)*

(enter an Old Man)

OLD MAN: Ah, Doctor Faustus, that I might prevail
To guide thy steps unto the way of life,
By which sweet path thou mayst attain the goal
That shall conduct thee to celestial rest!
Break heart, drop blood, and mingle it with
tears—
Tears falling from repentant heaviness
Of thy most vile and loathsome filthiness,
The stench whereof corrupts the inward soul
With such flagitious crimes of heinous sins
As no commiseration may expel
But mercy, Faustus, of thy Savior sweet,
Whose blood alone must wash away thy guilt.

FAUSTUS: Where are thou, Faustus? Wretch, what
hast thou done?

Damned art thou, Faustus, damned! Despair
and die.
Hell calls for right, and with a roaring voice
Says, "Faustus, come; thine hour is come!"
And Faustus will come to do thee right. *(Mephis-
tophilis gives him a dagger)*

OLD MAN: Ah stay, good Faustus, stay thy desperate
steps!
I see an angel hovers o'er thy head,
And with a vial full of precious grace,
Offers to pour the same into thy soul:
Then call for mercy and avoid despair.

FAUSTUS: Ah my sweet friend, I feel thy words
To comfort my distressed soul.
Leave me awhile to ponder on my sins.

OLD MAN: I go, sweet Faustus, but with heavy
cheer,
Fearing the ruin of thy hopeless soul. *(exit)*

FAUSTUS: Accursed Faustus, where is mercy now?
I do repent and yet I do despair:
Hell strives with grace for conquest in my
breast.
What shall I do to shun the snares of death?

MEPH: Thou traitor, Faustus, I arrest thy soul
For disobedience to my sovereign lord.
Revolt, or I'll in piecemeal tear thy flesh.

FAUSTUS: Sweet Mephistophilis, entreat thy lord
To pardon my unjust presumption,
And with my blood again I will confirm
My former vow I made to Lucifer.

MEPH: Do it then quickly with unfeigned heart
Lest greater danger do attend thy drift.

FAUSTUS: Torment, sweet friend, that base and
crooked age*
That durst dissuade me from thy Lucifer,
With greatest torments that our hell affords.

MEPH: His faith is great: I cannot touch his soul;
But what I may afflict his body with
I will attempt, which is but little worth.

FAUSTUS: One thing, good servant, let me crave of
thee
To glut the longing of my heart's desire:
That I might have unto my paramour
That heavenly Helen which I saw of late,
Whose sweet embracings may extinguish clean
These thoughts that do dissuade me from my
vow,
And keep mine oath I made to Lucifer.

MEPH: Faustus, this, or what else thou shalt desire
Shall be performed in twinkling of an eye.

(enter Helen)

FAUSTUS: Was this the face that launched a
thousand ships
And burnt the topless towers of Ilium?
Sweet Helen, make me immortal with a kiss.
Her lips suck forth my soul—see where it flies!
Come, Helen, come, give me my soul again.
Here will I dwell, for heaven is in these lips
And all is dross that is not Helena.

(enter Old Man who silently looks on)

I will be Paris, and for love of thee
Instead of Troy shall Wittenberg be sacked,
And I will combat with weak Menelaus

---

*crooked age: i.e., the old man

And wear thy colors on my plumed crest;
Yea, I will wound Achilles in the heel
And then return to Helen for a kiss.
O thou art fairer than the evening air
Clad in the beauty of a thousand stars!
Brighter art thou than flaming Jupiter
When he appeared to hapless Semele,
More lovely than the monarch of the sky
In wanton Arethusa's azured arms,
And none but thou shalt be my paramour! *(exit
all except the Old Man)*

OLD MAN: Accursed Faustus, miserable man,
That from thy soul excludest the grace of
heaven
And fliest the throne of his tribunal seat.

(enter the Devils to torment him)

Satan begins to sift me with his pride.
As in this furnace God shall try my faith,
My faith, vile hell, shall triumph over thee!
Ambitious fiends, see how the heavens smiles
At your repulse, and laughs your state to scorn.
Hence, hell! for hence I fly unto my God. *(exit)*

SCENE 12

Enter Faustus with the Scholars.

FAUSTUS: Ah, gentlemen!

1ST SCHOLAR: What ails Faustus?

FAUSTUS: Ah, my sweet chamber-fellow, had I lived with thee then had I lived still, but now I die eternally. Look! comes he not? comes he not?

2ND SCHOLAR: What means Faustus?

3RD SCHOLAR: Belike he is grown into some sickness by being over-solitary.

1ST SCHOLAR: If it be so, we'll have physicians to cure him; 'tis but a surfeit, never fear, man.

FAUSTUS: A surfeit of deadly sin that hath damned both body and soul.

2ND SCHOLAR: Yet, Faustus, look up to heaven: remember God's mercies are infinite.

FAUSTUS: But Faustus' offense can ne'er be pardoned; the Serpent that tempted Eve may be saved, but not Faustus. Ah, gentlemen, hear me with patience, and tremble not at my speeches. Though my heart pants and quivers to remember that I have been a student here these thirty years, O would I had never seen Wittenberg, never read book! And what wonders I have done all Germany can witness, yea all the world, for which Faustus hath lost both Germany and the world, yea heaven itself—heaven the seat of God, the throne of the blessed, the kingdom of joy, and must remain in hell forever, hell, ah hell, forever! Sweet friends, what shall become of Faustus, being in hell forever?

3RD SCHOLAR: Yet, Faustus, call on God.

FAUSTUS: On God, whom Faustus hath abjured? on God, whom Faustus hath blasphemed? Ah, my God, I would weep, but the Devil draws in my tears! Gush forth, blood, instead of tears, yea, life and soul. O he stays my tongue; I would lift up my hands but, see, they hold them, they hold them!

ALL: Who, Faustus?

FAUSTUS: Lucifer and Mephistophilis. Ah, gentlemen, I gave them my soul for my cunning.

ALL: God forbid!

FAUSTUS: God forbade it indeed, but Faustus hath done it: for vain pleasure of twenty-four years hath Faustus lost eternal joy and felicity. I writ them a bill with mine own blood, the date is expired, the time will come, and he will fetch me.

1ST SCHOLAR: Why did not Faustus tell us of this before, that divines might have prayed for thee?

FAUSTUS: Oft have I thought to have done so, but the Devil threatened to tear me in pieces if I named God, to fetch both body and soul if I once gave ear to divinity; and now 'tis too late. Gentlemen, away, lest you perish with me.

2ND SCHOLAR: O what shall we do to save Faustus?

66

FAUSTUS: Talk not of me, but save yourselves and depart.

3RD SCHOLAR: God will strengthen me: I will stay with Faustus.

1ST SCHOLAR: Tempt not God, sweet friend, but let us into the next room, and there pray for him.

FAUSTUS: Ay, pray for me, pray for me! And what noise soever ye hear, come not unto me, for nothing can rescue me.

2ND SCHOLAR: Pray thou, and we will pray that God may have mercy upon thee.

FAUSTUS: Gentlemen, farewell. If I live till morning I'll visit you; if not, Faustus is gone to hell.

ALL: Faustus, farewell. *(exit Scholars)*

(the clock strikes eleven)

FAUSTUS: Ah, Faustus,
Now hast thou but one bare hour to live
And then thou must be damned perpetually!
Stand still, you ever-moving spheres of heaven,
That time may cease and midnight never come;
Fair Nature's eye, rise, rise again, and make
Perpetual day; or let this hour be but
A year, a month, a week, a natural day,
That Faustus may repent and save his soul! -
*O lente lente currite noctis equi.**
The stars move still, time runs, the clock will
  strike,
The Devil will come, and Faustus must be
  damned.
O I'll leap up to my God! Who pulls me down?

lente lente currite noctis equi: "run slowly, slowly, horses of the night," a quotation from Ovid

67

See, see, where Christ's blood streams in the
   firmament!—
One drop would save my soul—half a drop! ah,
   my Christ!
Ah, rend not my heart for naming of my Christ;
Yet will I call on him—Oh, spare me, Lucifer!
Where is it now? 'Tis gone; and see where God
Stretcheth out his arm and bends his ireful
   brows.
Mountains and hills, come, come and fall on me
And hide me from the heavy wrath of God.
No, no—
Then will I headlong run into the earth:
Earth, gape! O no, it will not harbor me.
You stars that reigned at my nativity,
Whose influence hath allotted death and hell,
Now draw up Faustus like a foggy mist
Into the entrails of yon laboring cloud
So that my soul may but ascend to heaven.

(the clock strikes)

Ah, half the hour is past;
'Twill all be past anon.
O God,
If thou wilt not have mercy on my soul,
Yet for Christ's sake whose blood hath
   ransomed me
Impose some end to my incessant pain:
Let Faustus live in hell a thousand years,
A hundred thousand, and at last be saved!
O, no end is limited to damned souls.
Why wert thou not a creature wanting soul?
Or why is this immortal that thou hast?
Ah, Pythagoras' *metempsychosis**—were that true,

*Pythagoras' *metempsychosis:* the theory formulated by Pythagoras of
the transmigration of souls

68

This soul should fly from me, and I be changed
Unto some brutish beast.
All beasts are happy, for when they die
Their souls are soon dissolved in elements,
But mine must live still to be plagued in hell.
Cursed be the parents that engendered me!
No, Faustus, curse thyself, curse Lucifer
That hath deprived thee of the joys of heaven.

(the clock strikes twelve)

O it strikes, it strikes! Now, body, turn to air
Or Lucifer will bear thee quick to hell. *(thunder
    and lightning)*
O soul, be changed into little water drops
And fall into the ocean, ne'er be found.
My God, my God, look not so fierce on me!

(thunder; enter Devils)

Adders and serpents, let me breathe awhile!
Ugly hell, gape not—come not, Lucifer—
I'll burn my books—ah, Mephistophilis!

(Mephistophilis exits with him)

(enter Chorus)

CHORUS: Cut is the branch that might have grown
    full straight,
And burned is Apollo's laurel bough
That sometime grew within this learned man.
Faustus is gone: regard his hellish fall,
Whose fiendful fortune may exhort the wise
Only to wonder at unlawful things
Whose deepness doth entice such forward wits
To practice more than heavenly power permits.
(exit)